MEMORY BOOSTER

Dr Shireen Stephen holds a Ph.D. in Health Psychology and an M.Phil. and M.Sc. in Applied Psychology. She is a counselling psychologist, researcher, writer and editor. She is well known for her episodic memory of remembering dates and connected events. She is also renowned for her auditory memory of remembering clients and their counselling sessions—even years later—without taking down any notes!

She has also authored *Smart Guide For Awesome Memory*, *The 4-Week Memory Challenge* and *Train Your Brain: Ultimate Memory Hacks*.

MEMORY BOOSTER
Brain Boosting Tips & Tricks

Shireen Stephen

RUPA

Published by
Rupa Publications India Pvt. Ltd 2019
7/16, Ansari Road, Daryaganj
New Delhi 110002

Sales Centres:

Allahabad Bengaluru Chennai
Hyderabad Jaipur Kathmandu
Kolkata Mumbai

ISBN: 978-93-5333-514-4

First impression 2019

10 9 8 7 6 5 4 3 2 1

The moral right of the author has been asserted.

Chapter 1

Introduction

Human beings have always been fascinated with puzzles and brain teasers. Archimedes was probably the first person in history to build a puzzle. It was known as the Loculus Archimedis, or Archemedes' Box, and was a cross between a jigsaw puzzle and a tangram. Historical records reveal that he enjoyed coming up with challenging problems for his peers to solve. Biblical kings such as Solomon and Hiram used to have riddle contests. More recently, famous writers such as Edgar Allan Poe, Lewis Carroll and J.R.R. Tolkien, entrepreneurs such as Leonardo da Vinci and Benjamin Franklin and architects such as Ernő Rubik have all been fascinated with developing and solving puzzles. This fascination continues today in the form of brain teasers in daily newspapers, quiz shows on television, game tournaments and of course, puzzle books.

Benefits of Puzzles

Puzzles and brain teasers have several benefits. The first major benefit is that solving puzzles keeps your brain mentally fit and strong. In children and adolescents, it can hone cognitive (thinking) abilities and can keep the brain sharp and agile. In adults, solving puzzles can help solve everyday problems more logically without stress and it also improves focus and concentration. In older adults, solving puzzles on a daily basis can keep the brain active and may also slow down the onset of brain degenerative diseases such as Parkinson's and Alzheimer's.

The second major benefit of solving puzzles on a daily basis is that it can translate to real-world problems as well. For example, just as you would solve a mathematical puzzle by using hard logic, you may be able to apply the same logic in a stressful situation either with your boss at work, a fast-approaching examination that you have not prepared for yet or a classmate who is bullying you. This not only makes life less stressful but makes problem-solving more enjoyable as well!

The third major advantage of solving puzzles is that it activates cognitive abilities that you might not otherwise use on a daily basis. This in turn activates different parts of your brain which help in improving your memory, your aptitude for problem-solving, your focus and attention, your reasoning skills, and your understanding and grasping abilities.

Puzzles also develop the three elements of intelligence: creativity, logic and analytical skills. They are a great means of conquering boredom, depression, anxiety and stress and can lead to personal discovery, motivation, self-control and satisfaction. Just as you need to keep your body physically fit and healthy, you also need to keep your mind active to improve the health of your brain. Solving puzzles, brain teasers and riddles for at least half an hour on a daily basis is all it takes to succeed in keeping your mind healthy and fit!

Cognitive Functions

Simply put, cognition is thinking, and it encompasses the processes associated with perception, knowledge, problem-solving, judgement, language and memory. Your brain has various cognitive functions. You may be more proficient in one area but may need some practice in another. Since different parts of your brain are responsible for specific cognitive functions, it is imperative to train these areas of your brain in order to boost your brain's performance. This can be done by solving puzzles and brain games that are specially designed to boost these specific areas of your brain.

The puzzles and brain games in this book test and train five aspects of cognitive functions listed below.

1. Logical thinking: helps you think in a disciplined way, basing your thoughts on facts and evidence.
2. Analytical thinking: helps hone your powers of deduction, problem-solving and reasoning.
3. Verbal reasoning: trains your language and comprehension, vocabulary, reading, etc.
4. Lateral thinking: helps you think creatively and find out-of-the-box solutions to problems.
5. Spatial memory: helps improve visualizations as well as the ability to transform and manipulate spatial figures mentally.

How to Use This Book

This book is chock-full of games, secret codes, brain teasers, puzzles, riddles and many more fun activities, all designed to boost the power of your brain to make it fit and active. It consists of five chapters that test and train a particular cognitive function of the brain. Each chapter consists of exercises with increasing levels of difficulty starting at beginner's level and moving on to expert level. The difficulty levels are indicated in each exercise as follows:

* Easy level
** Intermediate level
*** Advanced level
**** Expert level

Each exercise takes about 10–20 minutes to solve. Try and complete at least one exercise per day. You can either choose to move from one chapter to the next, working through the puzzles and exercises in a systematic way by training one cognitive function at a time; or you can choose to do one exercise in each chapter, which will train different cognitive functions simultaneously. However, it is recommended that you start with the beginner-level exercises and work your way through the tougher levels in each chapter. Answers are provided at the back of the book.

Chapter 2

Just Deduce it!

When we say that something is logical, what we actually mean is that it makes sense. Logical thinking is the process in which one uses reasoning and cold, hard facts consistently to come to a conclusion. It may also involve combining a set of premises to reach a logical conclusion. For example, if A = B and B = C, then logically, C = A. Enhancing logical reasoning is simply learning to pay closer attention to details. Logic requires no prior knowledge, no mathematical or linguistic skills—just the ability to use reason in a logical way. Honing this skill improves your powers of observation and deduction.

Exercise 1: Relative Relationships*

1. Ann runs faster than Nikki
    Nikki runs faster than Jemma.
    Ann runs faster than Jemma.

    If the first two statements are true, then the third statement is:
    True   False   Uncertain

2. Mr Smith has four daughters. Each of his daughters has a brother. How many children does Mr Smith have?

3. Which statement is false?
    a) Statement D is true.
    b) Statement A is false.

    c)   Statement B is false.

    d)   Statement C is true.

4.   Jane and Jemima are called Stephen and Jones, but it is unclear if it is Jane Stephen and Jemima Jones or Jane Jones and Jemima Stephen. Given that two of the following statements are false, what is Jane's surname?

    a)   Jane's surname is Jones.

    b)   Jane's surname is Stephen.

    c)   Jemima's surname is Stephen.

5.   Using the following clues, place the letters between A and I in the grid below. Hint: 'Above/below' refers to two letters in the same column. 'Left/right' refers to two letters in the same row.

    a)   C is below G and above E

    b)   D is above A and to the right of F

    c)   F is above I and to the left of D

    d)   A is above H and to the right of I

    e)   H is to the right of B and to the left of E

6.   There is only one correct answer among the following answers. Which is it?

    a)   Answer A

    b)   Answer A and B

    c)   Answer B and C

7. Paul is taller than Jerry
   Bob is shorter than Paul

   Which of the following statements do you know for certain?
   a) Jerry is taller than Bob
   b) Bob is taller than Jerry
   c) It cannot be determined if Bob or Jerry is tallest

8. Four friends were sharing a pizza. They decided that the oldest friend would get the extra piece. Radha is two months older than Georgie, who is three months younger than Priya. Kelly is one month older than Georgie. Who should get the extra piece of pizza?
   a) Radha
   b) Georgie
   c) Priya
   d) Kelly

9. Four people were painting Mr. Cree's house. Sam is painting the front of the house. Ronny is in the alley behind the house painting the back. Joseph is painting the window frames on the north side, Kiran is on the south. If Sam switches places with Joseph, and Joseph then switches places with Kiran, where is Kiran?
   a) In the alley behind the house
   b) On the north side of the house
   c) On the south side of the house
   d) In front of the house

10. Last night, Priya and her husband invited their friends (two couples) to dinner. The six of them sat at a round table. Priya narrates the following:

- George sat on the left of the woman who sat on the left of the man who sat on the left of Asha.
- Preethi sat on the left of the man who sat on the left of the woman who sat on the left of the man who sat on the left of the woman who sat on the left of my husband.
- Pradeep sat on the left of the woman who sat on the left of Dilip.
- I did not sit beside my husband.

Where is each person sitting? What is the name of Priya's husband?

Hint: It may help if you draw the round table and place each person at their seats.

Exercise 2: Disconnect Four**

1. Draw either an X or an O in every empty space in the following grid taking care not to have any lines of four or more Xs or Os either horizontally, vertically or diagonally.

X				O	O		O
	O		X				X
		O	O		X		X
O	X	O		O			O
O						X	
	X		X		X	X	X
		X		O			X
X			O	O			O

2. The following puzzle is slightly different from the one above. Fill up all squares with Xs and Os. All rows and columns need to have four Xs and four Os however, there must not be more than **two** of the same letter in direct succession. For example, a row with XXOOXOOXO is valid but a row with XXXOOXOO is invalid because of the three Xs. This rule is valid only horizontally and vertically but not diagonally (it's okay to have more than two Xs or Os diagonally).

X	X		X			O	
X	X	O				X	
			O				
				O	X		O
O		O	O				
				X			
	X				O	X	X
	O			X		X	X

Exercise 3: Tricky Logic**

The answers to the following questions are not as straightforward as they seem. Read the questions carefully before answering.

1. A man wants to enter an exclusive club, but he doesn't know the password. Another man walks to the door and the doorman says twelve. The man says six, and

is let in. Another man walks up and the doorman says six. The man says three, and is let in. Thinking he has heard enough, he walks up to the door and the doorman says ten. He says five, and he isn't let in. What should he have said?

2. In the centre of a round lake lies a beautiful lotus. The lotus doubles in size every day. After exactly twenty days, the lotus covers the whole lake. How many days would it have taken the lotus to cover half the lake?

3. Two men were born at the same time. They both grew up, travelled the world and died at the same time. However, they did not live to the same age. How?

4. Paul and Martha are married and have two children, one of whom is a girl. Assuming that the probability of each gender is 1/2, what is the probability that the other child is also a girl?

5. An Arab sheikh tells his two sons to race their camels to a distant city to see who will inherit his fortune. The one whose camel is slower wins. After wandering aimlessly for days, the brothers ask a wise man for guidance. Upon receiving the advice, they jump on the camels and race to the city as fast as they can. What did the wise man say to them?

6. Three disciples wanted to find out who was the wisest amongst them so they turned to their leader, asking him to resolve their dispute. Their leader told them that he would blindfold all of them and paint either a red or a blue dot on each man's forehead. 'When I take your blindfolds off,' he said, 'if you see at least one red dot on another man's forehead, you must raise your hand. The one who guesses the colour of the dot on his own forehead first wins.'

The leader blindfolded his three disciples and painted red dots on all of them. When he took their blindfolds off, all three men raised their hands as the rules required, and sat in silence, pondering. Finally, one of them said, 'I have a red dot on my forehead.'

How did he know?

7. There are three switches on the ground floor. Each switch corresponds to one of the three light bulbs on the first floor, which you cannot see. You can turn the switches on and off or leave them in any position. How would you identify which switch corresponds to which light bulb, if you are only allowed one trip upstairs?

8. A family of two parents and two children (a son and a daughter) need to cross a river that has no bridge. The only way to get to the other side is to ask a nearby fisherman if he can lend him his boat. However, the boat is very small and can either carry one adult or two children at a time. How does the family get to the other side and then return the boat to the fisherman?

9. If the following list is a list of ten words, logically, what would the first two words be?

_____

_____

Third
Fourth
Fifth
Sixth
Seventh
Eighth
Ninth
Tenth

10. What letter can you place on the line below to form a complete word?

S E Q U E N C _

Exercise 4: What comes next?*****

Look at the sequences of boxes below and logically work out what figure should come next. Choose your answer from options A to E. Each question may require a different kind of logic in order to solve it.

1.

A   B   C   D   E

2.

A   B   C   D   E

3.

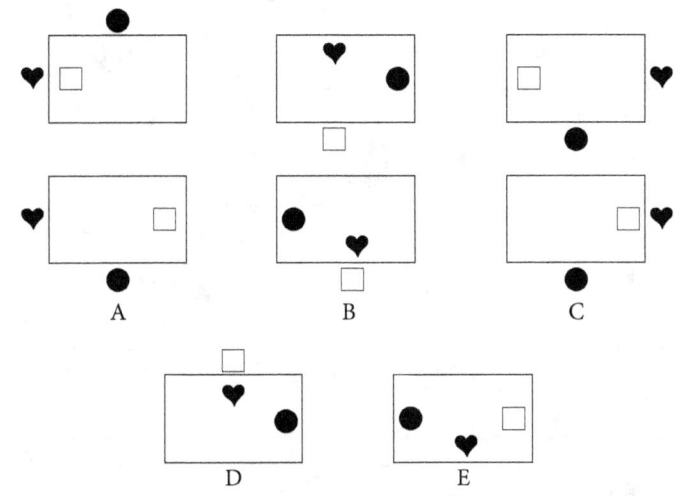

4.

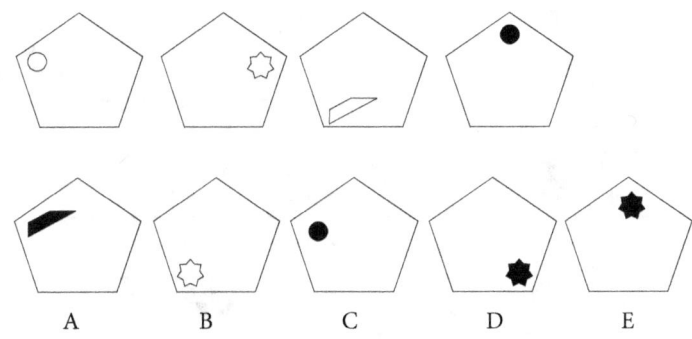

5.

6.

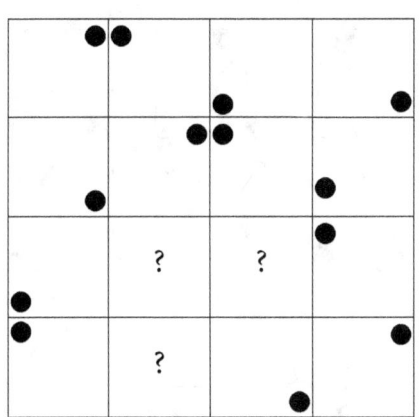

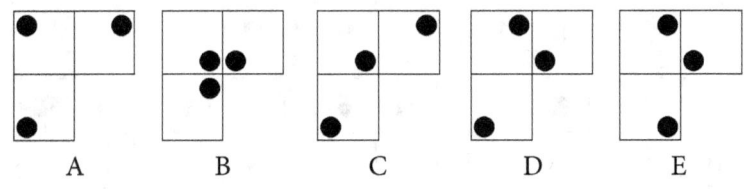

| A | B | C | D | E |

7.

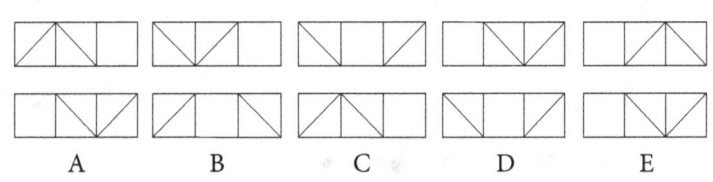

| A | B | C | D | E |

8.

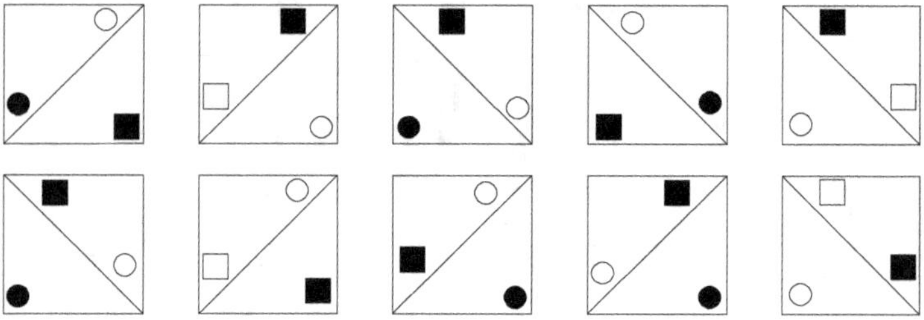

9.

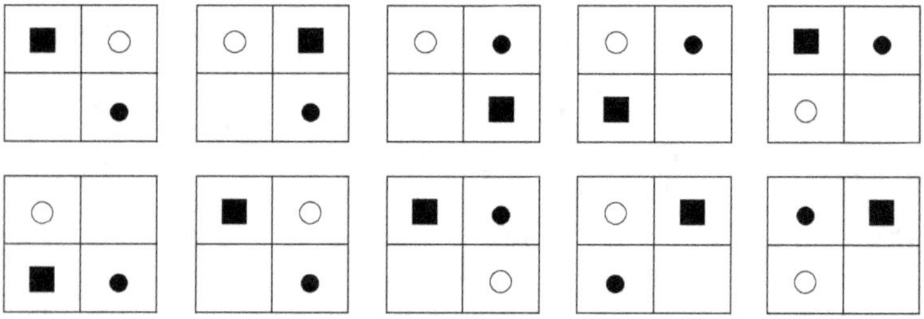

10.

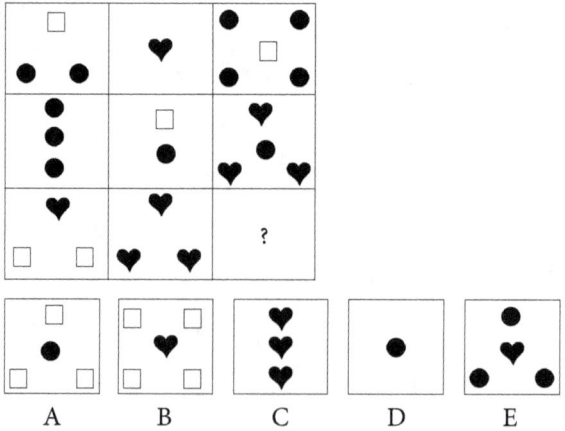

Chapter 3

Analyse This!

Analytical thinking involves thinking about things in a critical way before arriving at the solution. People with strong analytical skills have the ability to investigate a problem methodically and arrive at a solution in a timely, efficient manner. They also have the ability to use clear, logical steps and make sound judgements based on hard facts before executing an action.

In this chapter, a problem may be presented to you with just a few clues that by themselves might not lead to the solution. You will need to analyse these clues by applying logic, which will then lead you to the solution. Analytical thinking helps you understand the cause and effect of certain phenomena and hones your deductive reasoning skills.

Exercise 1: Elementary, my dear Watson*

You are provided with a few clues to the following mysteries. Put your detective cap on and see if you can deduce and solve all the mysteries.

1. A man was shot dead in his car. There were no powder marks on his clothing, which indicated that the murderer was outside the car. However, all the windows were up and all the doors were locked, with the key still in the ignition. How was he murdered?
2. An undercover detective had infiltrated an oil smuggling ring. However, just a day before he was going to bust the

gang, he goes missing. Before he disappeared, he had the presence of mind to leave a note for you: 710 57735 34, 5508 51 7718. You have four suspects: Bill, John, Todd and Luke. Can you break the detective's code and find out which of your four suspects is the culprit?

3. Luke was kidnapped and the kidnappers sent a ransom note to his family asking for one lakh rupees in unmarked notes. The money was to be put into a suitcase and kept under a bench in a nearby park. Luke's brother Thomas was to place the suitcase under the park bench at 8 o'clock sharp that night. However, while he was on his way to the bench, somebody hit him on his head from behind and ran away with the suitcase. When you questioned him, Thomas said, 'It was very dark in the park but I managed to see the attacker. He had red hair, was wearing a V-neck sweater and baggy blue jeans.' You immediately arrest Thomas on suspicion of kidnapping his own brother. What made you suspect him?

4. You are kidnapped and locked in a room with two other people. All three of you have a number written on your foreheads. None of you know what number it is. The first man has the number two written on his forehead while the second man has the number three written on his. The kidnapper tells you that the number on one of your foreheads is the sum of the other two numbers. Each number is unique. You can't talk to each other and you cannot use sign language or any means of communication. If you guess your own number, you will be set free. What number is on your forehead?

5. An elderly gentleman named Jack lived alone. Because of his old age, he couldn't leave his house. So, he had everything delivered to him, including his milk, mail,

newspapers and groceries. One Tuesday, the mailman went to deliver the letters and found the front door ajar. On pushing it open, he found Jack sprawled on the living-room floor, dead. He immediately called you, the police. When you arrive, you notice two bottles of milk, Monday's newspaper, a small bag of groceries, two unopened letters and some brochures on the front porch. You immediately have a suspect. Who do you arrest?

6. In a tourist village that is currently hosting gypsies, nomads, Celtic tribes and circus folk, a local shopkeeper is found dead just outside his shop. He had time to scrawl the following cryptic numbers in the sand outside before he died: 11-10-3-8-12-9. Which group do you think killed the shopkeeper?

7. Your grandfather is telling you war stories. 'At the end of World War I, I was awarded for my bravery after saving a group of my men,' he says. 'You see, we were fighting in northern France and one of our enemies threw a grenade at us. I managed to pick it up and throw it away before it exploded. So, right after the war ended, a general gave me a sword, engraved with the words "Awarded for Bravery and Valour, A True Hero, World War I."' You think about the story for a minute and then say, 'Grandpa, that story can't be true!' How do you know?

8. A man at a party was extremely thirsty and gulped down some of the freshly made iced fruit punch. Being an introvert, he left the party early. Everyone at the party who drank the fruit punch subsequently died of poisoning. Why did the man not die?

9. Margaret was found dead in her living room by Edith. Edith recounted her horrifying discovery to you, the detective on the crime scene. 'I was walking by Margaret's

house when I thought I would just pop in for a visit. I noticed her living room light on and I decided to peek in to see if she was in there. There was frost on the window, so I had to wipe it away to see inside. That is when I saw her body. I kicked in the front door immediately to try and save her but she was already dead by then. I called the police immediately afterward.'

You immediately arrested Edith for murdering Margaret. How did you know that Edith was lying?

10. There are five people. One of them shot one of the five. With the help of the following clues, find out who the murderer is and who the victim is.

- Sam ran a marathon yesterday with one of the innocent men.
- George was a farmer before he moved to the city.
- Ross is a top-notch computer consultant and is going to install Kevin's new computer next week.
- The murderer had his leg amputated last month.
- Kevin met Ricky for the first time six months ago.
- Ricky has been in seclusion since the crime.
- Sam used to drink heavily.
- Kevin and Ross built their last computers together.
- The murderer is Ricky's brother. They grew up together.

Exercise 2: Shorthand**

The following are abbreviations of common phrases. Try and figure them out. For example, 24 H in a D may be short for '24 hours in a day'.

1. 26 L of the A
2. 7 W of the W
3. 12 S of the Z

4. 52 C in a P (W/OJs)
5. 1000 Y in a M
6. 90 D in a R A T
7. 3 B M (S H T R)
8. 29 D in F in a L Y
9. 13 L in a B D
10. 9 L of a C

Exercise 3: Decoding Riddles!***

This is an exercise in decoding. It is twofold:
    a)   Using Morse code below, decode the riddles.
    b)   Only the riddle questions are given. Once you decode the questions, try and find an answer.

Hint: While you need analytical skills to decode the questions, the riddles themselves are downright silly and require out-of-the-box silly answers. For example, what did Cinderella wear to the beach? Glass flippers, of course!

Morse Code

A	.-	K	-.-	U	..-
B	-...	L	.-..	V	...-
C	-.-.	M	- -	W	.- -
D	-..	N	-.	X	-..-
E	.	O	- - -	Y	-.- -
F	..-.	P	.- -.	Z	- - ..
G	- -.	Q	- -.-		
H	....	R	.-.		
I	..	S	...		
J	.- - -	T	-		

a) . - - . . . . . - . - -/- . - . - . . - - . -/- . - - - - - - . . -/ - . - . . . . - - ./
    . -/- . - . . - . . - - - - . - . - . -/. . - ./ . - - - . - . . . - . ?

b) . - - . . . . . - -/. . . . . - . . - . ./- . - . . . - . . . - - . . . . - ./- .
    . . . . - . . . -/- - . - - - . . . ./ - - - -/. - - - . - . . . . - . . ?

c) . - - . . . . . . - . ./- . . . - - -/ - - . . . - . - - - - . . . ./ . . . . - - .
    . - -?

d) . . . . - - - . - -/. - . . - . - - - - . - - ./ . . . . - - - - . . - . - .
    . - . ./ - . . . - - - - . - . - - - - . - . . ./ . - . - . - . . - - . - . . - .
    . - . - . . / - - . - . - . . . - . - . . . - . . ?

e) . - - . . . . . . - -/. . . . . ./- . . . ./. - . . . - - - - . . . . . -/. - - - .
    . - . - . -/- - - . . - . /. - / - . - . . - . - ?

f) . - - . . . . . - . - -/- . . . . . - . ./- . . . . . ./- . . . . - . / . .
    . - . . . - . - . /. - / - . . . . . - . - . . -/- - - . . . - . / . - - . . - . . .
    . - - . - - . - . . - - . /- . - . . . - . - . - . . . ?

g) . - - . . . . . . - ./ . . . . ./. .-/- - . . . - - ./. . - - - . - - . - . - . . . .
    . - - - - . - - . - . . ?

h) . - - . . . . . . - -/. . . . . . - . . ./. . - . - - - - . . . . - ./. - . . . - - .
    . . ./. - - . - . . ./. . - . . - . - - . . . . . . ?

i) . - - . . . . - . ./- . - . - - - . . . ./.-/- . - . - . - . . - . . - . ./. . - -?

j) . - - . . . . - . ./- . . . - - -/- . . - . . . - . - . . . ./. . . . - - . . - -?

Exercise 4: Einstein's Riddle****

The following riddle is said to have been created by Albert Einstein in the last century. Einstein said that only 2 per cent of the world's population can solve it. This puzzle requires pure logic and analytical skills. All the best!

There are five houses of different colours next to each other. In each house lives a man. Each man has a unique nationality, an exclusive favourite drink, a distinct favourite brand of cigarettes and keeps specific pets. Using all the clues below, fill up the grid and answer the question: 'Who owns the fish?'

Hint: Start with the questions that clearly state the position of the person's nationality, drink, cigarette, colour or pet.

- The Brit lives in the red house.
- The Swede keeps dogs as pets.
- The Dane drinks tea.
- The green house is next to the white house, on the left.
- The owner of the green house drinks coffee.
- The person who smokes Pall Mall rears birds.
- The owner of the yellow house smokes Dunhill.
- The man living in the house in the centre drinks milk.
- The Norwegian lives in the first house.
- The man who smokes Blends lives next to the man who keeps cats.
- The man who keeps horses lives next to the man who smokes Dunhill.
- The man who smokes Blue Master drinks beer.
- The German smokes Prince.
- The Norwegian lives next to the blue house.
- The man who smokes Blends has a neighbour who drinks water.

	House 1	House 2	House 3	House 4	House 5
Colour					
Nationality					
Drink					
Cigarette					
Pet					

Chapter 4

Word's Worth

Verbal reasoning is the ability to understand and logically work through concepts and problems expressed in words. A strong vocabulary helps you do better in school and in your profession as it aids your ability to think constructively, understand concepts and solve problems in logical or creative ways. Verbal reasoning tests are often used as entrance tests in schools and colleges to test an individual's aptitude. They are also used by employers as part of the recruitment process in job interviews.

Exercise 1: Word Games*

1. The first and last letters have been removed from the following words. Try and find out what they are in order to complete the word.

   Hint: The first and last letters are the same. For example, you can complete the word ___ I L L O ___ by adding a W on both ends.

   a) ___ I D O ___
   b) ___ H U N ___
   c) ___ E D I U ___
   d) ___ I V I ___
   e) ___ Y P I S ___
   f) ___ I T E R A ___
   g) ___ O U ___
   h) ___ E I N D E E ___
   i) ___ O T I O ___

j) ___ O I N ___

2. Find a common word that completes the first word and begins the next word. For example, 'night ___ ___ ___ ___ boat' can be solved using the word 'life' to get 'night life' and 'life boat.'

Hint: The number of dashes is the number of letters in the word.

a) sword ___ ___ ___ ___ finger
b) sweet ___ ___ ___ ___ flake
c) play ___ ___ ___ friend
d) honey ___ ___ ___ ___ beam
e) some ___ ___ ___ ___ armour
f) cat ___ ___ ___ ___ out
g) bird ___ ___ ___ ___ less
h) free ___ ___ ___ ___ cuffed
i) sir ___ ___ ___ ___ cloth
j) over ___ ___ ___ ___ ___ less

3. All the vowels (a, e, i, o, u) have been removed from the following American states. Try and replace all of them.

a) lbm
b) clrd
c) dlwr
d) llns
e) dh
f) mn
g) nvd
h) h
i) rgn
j) txs

4. The following are a list of superheroes from the Marvel comic books and movies. Find them by striking out pairs of unnecessary letters.

a) ASJEWESFSWFSSWIFGCPOAYT
   JRFOBMNEREESSTH
b) SWEPSDIPODQFEUFRTJMEPAVBNWD
c) ZUWVGOPLLEDVMLEEFRUVIOINWEE
d) WDUDBIERTAEDDNBPEYOILORFLR
e) HGIEERGGOIYNTYMESABHNR
f) AFGVEDEESNOIGTYERTREFS
g) HLEUUDFKEHE RTCEBAUJGERES
h) GTBEFLSFAEHCERKEG
   PETAOPNRTTNBHEREETRW
i) QECURAEVPRTTPOACVIERNUY
   AEDMMNEEUREDIZXCERAS
j) APWEMASDSERPVF

Exercise 2: Anagram Scramble**

Unscramble the following anagrams to find out the names of different countries.

1. A infant gash
2. Sly leeches
3. Blade hangs
4. A cob maid
5. Oh it a pie
6. Adios nine
7. Bugle rum ox
8. Raga scam ad
9. Handle rents
10. No Maria

Exercise 3: Across Words***

1. Find the first two letters and the last two letters of each word.
   Hint: The last two letters of each word are the first two letters of the next word.

		C	K	S	T		
		D	U	C	T		
		U	C	A	T		
		P	R	E	S		
		L	I	T	U		
		C	L	I	N		
		I	T	I	O		

2. The following is a word pyramid. Follow the clues to fill up the blanks.

   Hint: Each word has all the letters of the previous word plus one additional letter.

   a) Symbol for phosphor
   b) Never-ending mathematical value
   c) Tasty baked pastry
   d) Evergreen coniferous tree
   e) Backbone
   f) Long-billed game birds inhabiting marshy areas
   g) Richly coloured viola flowers

3. The following pairs of words are opposites of each other. Figure them out and place them in the correct boxes.
   a) TTPABNSNRES

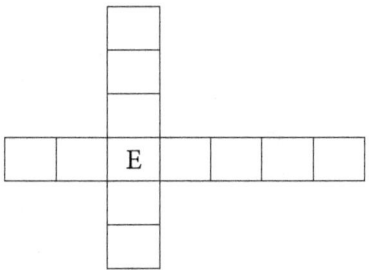

   b) NNINACTRODM

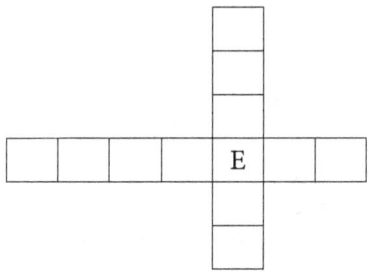

   c) VDDEELI

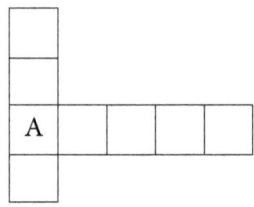

4. Unscramble the letters below to make one nine-letter word. Make as many words as you can that contain four letters and above. Each word must contain the highlighted letter. Time yourself. See if you can get over twenty words in two minutes or less for each of the words.

a)	U	Z	S	R	B	O	Z	W	D

b)	A	I	I	M	D	S	M	E	X

c)	Q	Z	N	E	G	S	I	U	E

5. Find the prefix (the word that comes before) to the following words.

   Hint: All the five words on the right have the same word on the left.

   a) ____ ____ ____ ____ ____   Conductor
   Man
   Structure
   Efficient
   Absorbent

   b) ____ ____ ____ ____ ____   Author
   Storey
   Task
   Plex
   Media

   c) ____ ____ ____ ____   Achieve
   Bearing
   Charge
   Cast
   Think

Exercise 4: Box Words****

Look at the individual boxes below and find words by starting with any letter and then moving left, right, up, down or diagonally to adjacent letters, without revisiting any square within a word. Try to find as many words as possible. There is one word that uses every letter in each box below. All words need to have four or more letters.

Hint: A minimum of 7 words, 28 words and 127 words can be found for boxes 1, 2 and 3, respectively. All words need to have four letters and above and there must be at least one word that uses every letter in the box.

1.

G	E	D
G	Z	G
A	Z	I

2.

E	J	B	S
T	C	U	L
I	V	E	Y

3.

E	N	I	T
D	D	M	N
N	S	A	E
E	S	S	B

Chapter 5

Figure It Out

Numerical reasoning is the ability to deal with numbers quickly and accurately. Numerical reasoning tests not only test and train your basic mathematical abilities but also your ability to use numerical data as a tool to make reasoned decisions and solve problems. These tests contain questions that assess your knowledge of percentages, number sequences and data interpretation and makes use of your logic and analytical skills.

This chapter contains four main exercises in numerical reasoning, only a few of which require mathematical calculations. The rest of the exercises require manipulation of numbers in a logical sequence or placement of numbers (or shading of boxes or drawing lines) according to pre-established rules.

Exercise 1: Simple Math*

1. What percentage of this grid is black and what percentage is white?

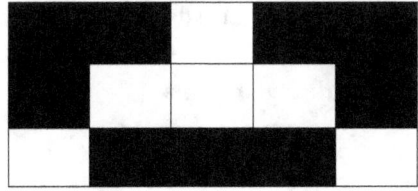

2. Which is the lower figure—the square root of 3 or the cube root of 5?
3. In a deck of playing cards, what is the sum of all the number cards?

4. Which of the following numbers are not prime numbers?

   3 13 23 33 73 113 143 173

5. Which three consecutive numbers can be multiplied to equal 1716?

6. Fill in the boxes in this mini sudoku so that each row and each column have the numbers 1,2,3 and 4 in them without repeating a number. The darker 2 x 2 boxes also need to have all four numbers in them without repeating any number.

		2	4
4	3		

7. The number of pairs of socks in a drawer is between 50 and 60. If you count them three at a time, you will find that there are two pairs left over. If you count them five at a time, you will find that there are four pairs left over. How many pairs of socks are there in the drawer?

8. Sophie works every second day at a supermarket and Stephie works every third day at the same supermarket. The supermarket is open on all seven days of the week. This week, Sophie started work on Tuesday, 1 December, and Stephie started work on Wednesday, 2 December. On what day will both of them work together next?

9. What number comes next?

   852 : 42

   756 : 36

   469 : ?

10. One number from the top needs to replace one number from the bottom and vice versa. Which two numbers in the

two sequences below need to be swapped? What is the logic behind the sequence?

20, 19, 17, 16, 14, 12

20, 18, 17, 15, 14, 13

Exercise 2: Deadly sequences**

Look at the sequences below and logically deduce what number replaces the question mark at the end.

Hint: Each question makes use of a different logical sequence.

1. 8723, 3872, 2387, **?**
2. 35, 57, 86, 25, 756, 65, 75, 26, 875, **?**
3. 25, 10, 35, 15, 50, **?**, **?**
4. 237 (13), 349 (21), 826 (**?**)
5. 440, 436, 433, 430, 427, **?**
6. 27, 82, 41, 124, 62, 31, 94, 47, 142, 71, **?**, **?**
7. 77, 143, 221, 323, **?**
8. 8, 12,24, 60, **?**
9. 1, 5, 32, 288, **?**
10. 6, 9, 27, 54, **?**, 2241

Exercise 3: Questioning Question Marks***

1. What number should replace the question mark?

634	97
543	**?**

2. What number should replace the question mark?

5	5
5	2

6	8
7	5

?	7
6	4

3. What letters should replace the question marks?

B	X
D	V
?	?
H	R
J	P
L	N

4. What number should replace the question mark?

9		7		8		8		7		4
	5				3				6	
6		5		4		9		3		?

5. What number should replace the question mark?

20	27	36

4	3	6

5	9	?

6. What number should replace the question mark?

5	7	3	6
2	78	61	4
1	?	29	4
8	9	2	3

7. What number should replace the question mark?

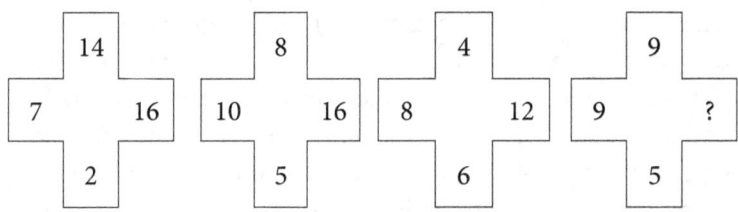

8. The top set of six numbers has a relationship with the set of six numbers below. By working out the relationship of the block of numbers to the left, try and figure out what numbers should replace the questions marks on the right.

2	5	4	9	8	3		13	26	19	32	23	18
1	6	3	10	7	4		?	?	?	?	?	?

9. What number should replace the question mark?

1	2	3
	9	
5	6	7

6	7	8
	2	
1	7	2

2	3	4
	2	
6	7	9

?	6	8
	1	
7	7	2

10. Each set of nine numbers relate to each other in a certain way. Work out the missing numbers on the right by working out the logic behind the numbers on the left.

3	7	9
4	3	1
8	1	0

5	7	6
?	?	?
9	0	5

Exercise 4: Placement Puzzles**

Placement puzzles may ask you to shade in squares, draw lines to form pathways, draw outlines or place numbers in a grid in a logical sequence. While these puzzles do not require any particular mathematical calculations, they do require precision, logic and analytical thinking. Take a few minutes to understand the puzzles and what is required of you before attempting them.

1. Nonogram: Shade in some squares on the grid below following the clues given outside the grid. Each number outside the grid depicts the number of consecutive squares that need to be shaded in that particular row or column. For example, if the number at the top is 2, it means that that column has 2 consecutively shaded squares. If the number on the side is 4, it means that that particular row has 4 consecutively shaded squares.

	2	4	6	8	10	4	4	4	4	4
1										
2										
3										
9										
10										
10										
9										
3										
2										
1										

2. Pathways: Fill the grid below with numbers from 1 to 64 so that each number forms a path within the grid, visiting each box only once. The numbers can be placed horizontally, vertically or diagonally in any direction.

					5	9	
		59	1		19		
	63			20			12
36			32			17	
			55		23		14
39		42		54			15
			53			29	
44				51		26	

3. Reverse minesweeper: The clues in the following puzzle tells you the number of mines surrounding it. For example, if the number is 2, it means that there are two mines in the adjacent squares surrounding the number 2. You need to either shade in the mines or mark them with an X.

   Hint: There might be a few blank squares as well (squares that don't have mines or numbers).

	1			1			1		
2		2		2				2	
	3		2		1	2			
		2		2			2		1
			1						1
					3			1	
		2		3		2			
	4				2			2	
2			4	2			2		
		2						4	

4. Infinite lines: The puzzle below is similar to reverse minesweeper. The numbers in the boxes depict how many surrounding boxes have lines running through them. You need to draw a single line through some of the empty boxes (lines cannot pass through numbered boxes) so that the line does not cross or overlap in any way. Lines can be either vertical or horizontal. A simple example is given below.

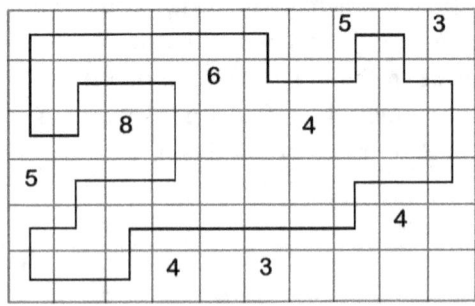

				3	2	4		
		7						
4		7		6		8		
								5
				7				
	5		7				6	
	5						4	
			7		5			
			4					

5. Carpeting: The following puzzle requires you to 'carpet' the area of the grid that is represented by specific numbers by shading in the required boxes. For example, if the number is 2, then two boxes (including the box with the number) need to be shaded. The catch is that only boxes that form rectangles or squares can be shaded—irregular shapes cannot be shaded. Also, no two 'carpets' can overlap each other. For example, Figure 1 below is wrong, while Figure 2 is correct. **Hint:** There can be blank boxes between carpets.

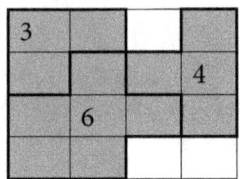

Figure 1

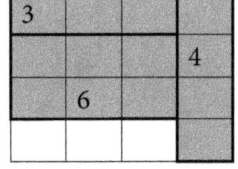

Figure 2

3			3				4		
		3				1		3	
				2	3	2			
2	3		4						4
				5			4		
	4		2						
			6		3			3	
				3	2				6
		4							
3	2				3		6		

Chapter 6

Space Sense

Spatial reasoning is the ability to perceive, analyse and understand simple and complex images, patterns and shapes. It is your ability to manipulate two- and three-dimensional shapes and your capacity to spot patterns or relationships between them. It is important in everyday life, work and science and plays a role in activities such as understanding metaphors, becoming good at navigating your way around new localities, interpreting works of art, solving jigsaw and other puzzles, planning business strategies, manipulating information in your mind, and in careers such as engineering, architecture, construction, design and astronomy.

Spatial ability involves creative and abstract reasoning combined with logical and analytical reasoning. Training and improving your spatial intelligence can help improve many functions of your brain including your cognitive abilities, memory, visualization skills, imagination and creativity, and problem-solving skills. It will also help you in cracking aptitude tests, IQ tests and interviews.

Exercise 1: Assembling Cubes*
How many of the following shapes can form three-dimensional cubes when they are folded?

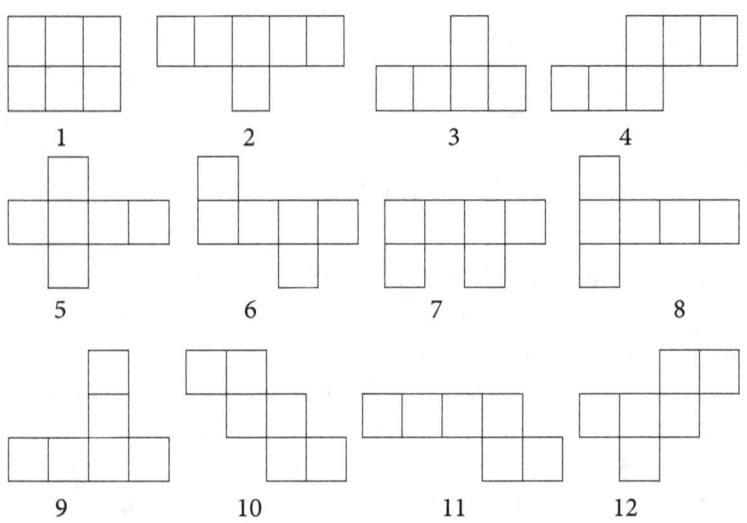

Exercise 2: Matchstick Moves**

1. Remove three matchsticks to form three squares.

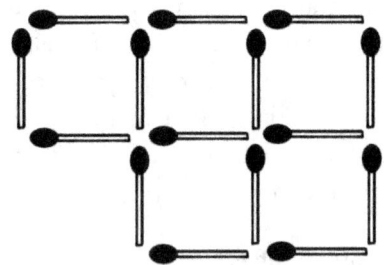

2. Remove four matchsticks to form five squares.

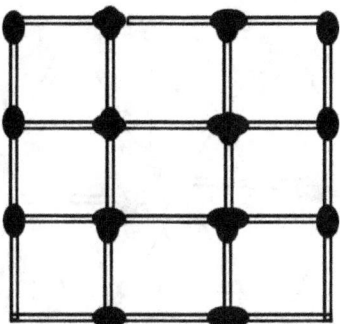

3. Move three matchsticks to form two squares.

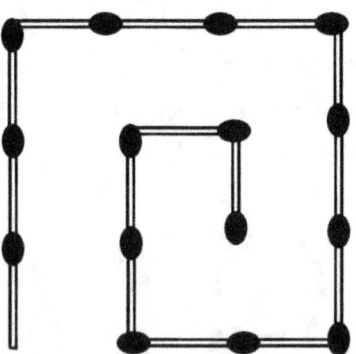

4. Here are three matchsticks. Without breaking them or adding any more, make them six.

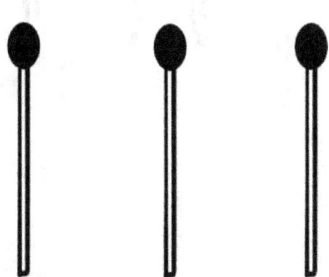

5. Move four matchsticks to form three equilateral triangles.

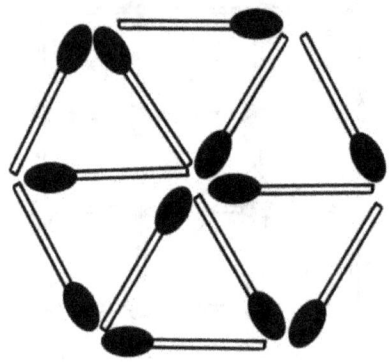

Exercise 3: Miscellaneous***

1. Here is a set of cogs connected by belts. If the top left cog is turned clockwise, in what direction will all the other cogs turn?

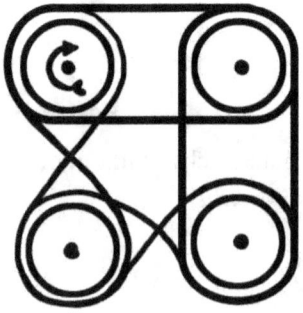

2. Which option is a replica of the image at the top?

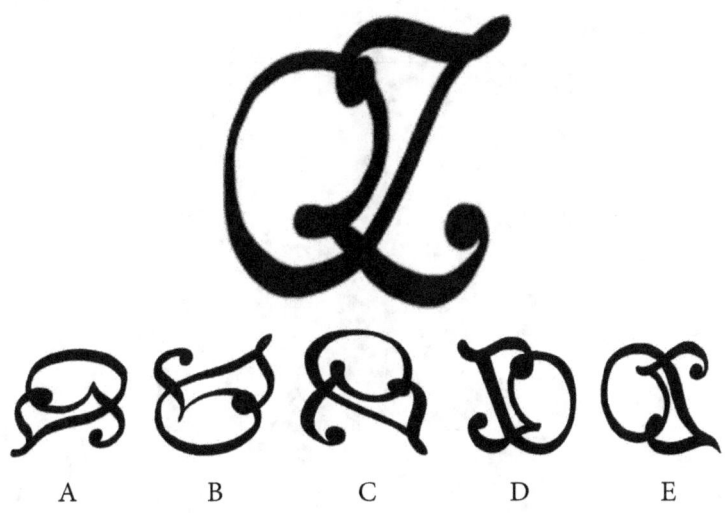

A	B	C	D	E

3. Which shape at the bottom can be assembled to form the shape on top?

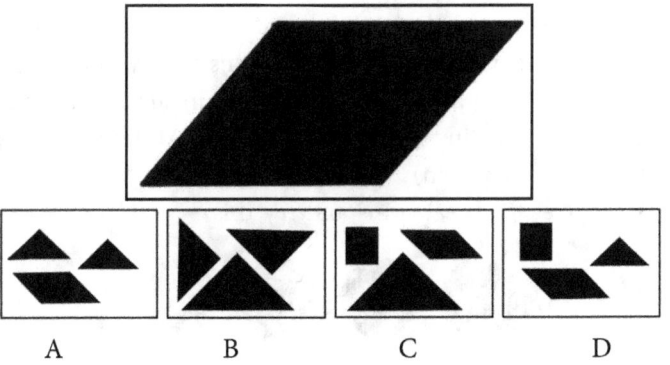

A	B	C	D

4. If you had to get the shape below by folding a square piece of paper and cutting it only once in a straight line, how would you do it??

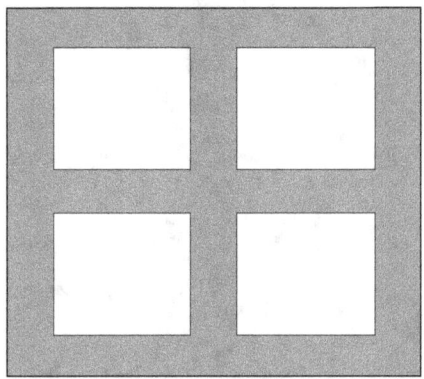

5. You have been invited to a party and have been asked to bring exactly 6 litres of juice. You have a 7-litre bottle full of juice and two empty bottles that are exactly 5 litres and 2 litres. Using the 7-litre, 5-litre and 2-litre bottles, how will you measure exactly 6 litres of juice to take with you?
6. Imagine that you have four round coins side by side, as shown below. Can you arrange the four coins in such a way that all coins are touching all the other coins? (All four coins have to touch every coin)
    Hint: Get four real coins and try this.

7. Look at the structure below and draw the shape from three views:
    a) Top view

b) Front view
c) Right view

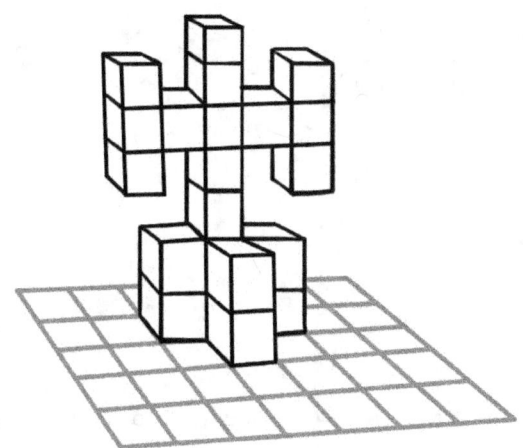

8. Which of the two images, A or B, will form the first image when folded?

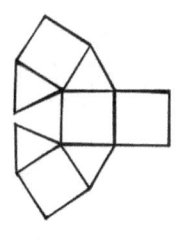

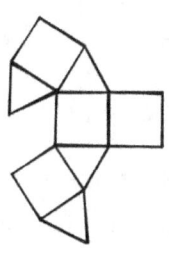

A   B

9. Each of the shapes below has an identical twin. Find the matching shape.

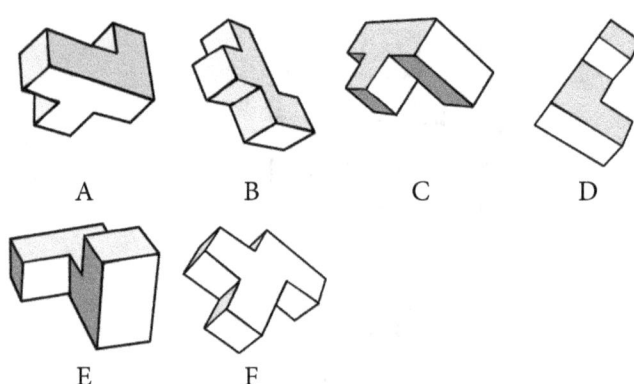

A   B   C   D

E   F

10. Which image, A, B or C, is identical to the first image?

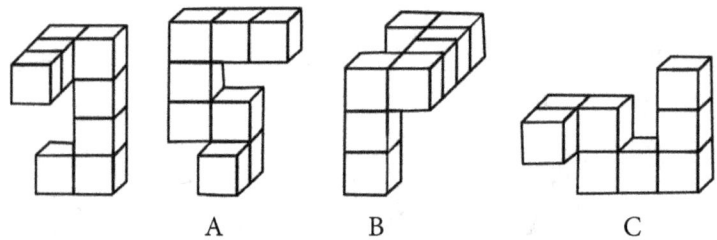

A   B   C

Exercise 4: Mirror Images**

A mirror image is an image or object which is identical to the original but with the structure reversed in some way. It is the original image as seen in a mirror. For example, if a mirror was placed on the right hand side of the number 7, the mirror image would be as follows:

In the following exercises, the 'mirror' will be placed either on top, bottom, right or left of the given image. Your task is to look at the original image for 60 seconds, then close the book and draw its mirror image.

1. The following is the Chinese symbol for 'angel'. Imagine that the mirror is on the right of the image, facing left.

天使

2. Draw the image below, imagining that the mirror is at the bottom, facing up.

3. Draw the image below, imagining that the mirror is on the left of the image, facing right.

4. Below is a picture of a multicoloured kite. Imagine that the mirror is at the top of it, facing downwards.

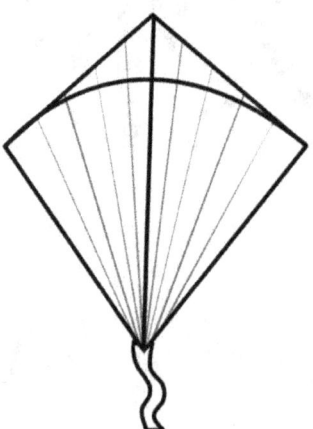

5. Draw the image below, imagining that the mirror is on its right.

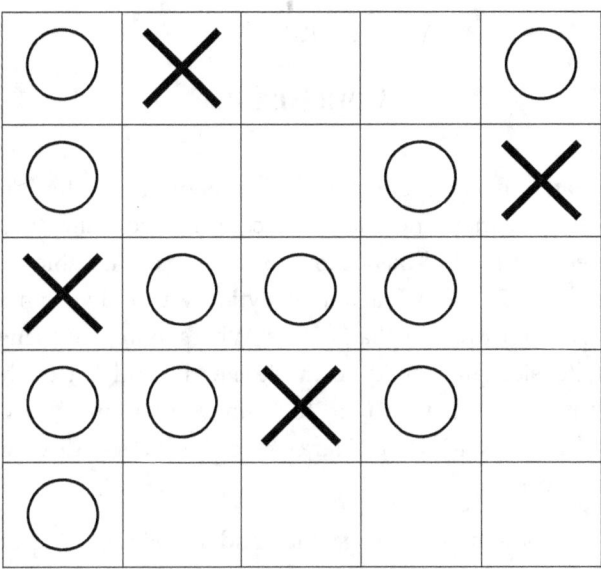

Chapter 7

Conclusion

Now that you have completed this book of brain boosting exercises, you may find that your concentration and focus has increased, your mind has become sharper, you are able to solve problems in a more logical and analytical way and your memory power is much stronger than before. What's more, your language, comprehension and ability to think laterally and out-of-the-box has also improved. Continue to train your brain by giving it more challenges to solve. Here are a few handy tips on how you can do this:

1. Scour newspapers, magazines and mobile applications for different types of puzzles, whether they are crosswords, sudoku (and variations such a kakuro, wordoku, windoku, picture sudoku, etc.) or other brain teasers. Once you become adept at a puzzle, try and step it up with more challenging versions of the same puzzle. Make sure that the challenges keep getting tougher and tougher until the toughest of problems is child's play to you.

2. You're never too old to go toy shopping! Whenever you pass a toy shop, go in and check out the latest toys, jigsaw puzzles and gadgets. Games such as darts, carom, chess, Chinese checkers, droughts and Legos are classics and help train various aspects of your cognitive abilities.

3. Console games and video games such as Super Mario, NeuroRacer, Need for Speed, etc. can stimulate neurogenesis

(growth of new neurons in the brain) and can stimulate spatial abilities, strategic planning, memory formation and fine motor movements.

4. Different software applications such as Lumosity, Elevate, Brain Training, Mental! and many more can be downloaded and installed on your mobile phone and can help with brain training.

5. Make solving puzzles a lifestyle change. Try to dedicate at least half an hour a day to solving puzzles. Once brain games become a part of your lifestyle, your mind will be sharp and agile all your life and what's more, your stress levels will decrease and your energy and vitality for life will increase. With an agile brain and a sharp mind, you will truly be a formidable force of nature.

All the very best!

Answers

CHAPTER 2

Just Deduce It!

Exercise 1: Relative Relationships*

1. True
2. Mr. Smith has 5 children—4 daughters and 1 son. Each daughter has the same brother.
3. Statement b) is false.
4. b) Jane's surname is Stephen.
5.

F	D	G
I	A	C
B	H	E

6. If answer 'a' is correct, then answer 'b' ('Answer A or B') would also be correct. If answer 'b' is correct, then answer 'c' ('Answer B or C') would also be correct. This leads to the conclusion that if either answer 'a' or answer 'b' are correct, there are at least two correct answers. This contradicts with the statement 'there is only one correct answer'. If answer 'c' is correct, then there are no contradictions. Therefore, the solution is answer 'c'.

7. Statement 'c' is certainly correct. The only thing that can be stated for sure is that Paul is the tallest. If Bob and Jerry have different heights, one of the other statements is also correct. However, if Bob and Jerry are of the same height, none of the other two statements are correct!

8. Priya is the oldest friend and should get the extra slice of pizza. If Radha is two months older than Georgie, then Priya is three months older than Georgie and one month older than Radha. Kelly is younger than both Radha and Priya. Therefore, Priya is the oldest.

9. Kiran is in front of the house. Ronny is in the alley behind the house, Sam is on the north side and Joseph is on the south.

10. From the second statement, we know that the six people sat at the table in the following way (clockwise and starting with Priya's husband):

    Priya's husband, woman, man, woman, man, Preethi

    Because Priya did not sit beside her husband, the situation must be as follows:

    Priya's husband, woman, man, Priya, man, Preethi

    The remaining woman must be Asha, and combining this with the first statement, we arrive at the following situation:

    Priya's husband, Asha, man, Priya, George, Preethi

    Because of the third statement, Pradeep and Dilip can be placed in only one way, and we now know the complete order:

    Priya's husband Dilip, Asha, Pradeep, Priya, George, Preethi

    Conclusion: The name of Priya's husband is Dilip.

Exercise 2: Disconnect Four**

1.

X	X	X	O	O	O	X	O
X	O	O	X	X	X	O	X
O	X	O	O	O	X	O	X
O	X	O	X	O	O	X	O
O	O	X	O	X	X	X	O
X	X	O	X	O	X	X	X
O	X	X	X	O	X	O	X
X	O	X	O	O	O	X	O

2.

X	X	O	X	O	X	O	O
X	X	O	X	O	O	X	O
O	O	X	O	X	X	O	X
X	O	X	X	O	X	O	O
O	X	O	O	X	O	X	X
X	O	X	O	X	X	O	O
O	X	O	X	O	O	X	X
O	O	X	O	X	O	X	X

Exercise 3: Tricky Logic**

1. The man should have said 3. The password is the number of letters in the number that the doorman says. Therefore, 'twelve' is 6, 'six' is 3 and 'ten' is also 3.
2. Nineteen days. Since the lotus doubles its size every day and the whole lake is filled in 20 days, half of the lake would have been covered one day earlier.

3. One went east, gaining in the number of days while the other went west, losing days.

4. No, the answer is not 1/2 as you would normally think. The answer is actually 1/3. The following are possible combinations:

    Girl – Girl

    Girl – Boy

    Boy – Girl

    Boy – Boy

    Since we already know that one of the children is a girl, this eliminates the Boy – Boy possibility. This leaves you with three possibilities, one of which is two girls. Therefore, the answer is 1/3.

5. The wise man told them to switch camels.

6. The following might have been the disciples' thinking process: 'All three of us (A, B, and C [me]) see everyone's hand up, which means that everyone can see at least one red dot on someone's head. If I (C) have a blue dot on my head, then both A and B see three hands up, one red dot (the only way they can raise their hands), and one blue dot (on my head). Therefore, A and B would both think this way: if the other guys' hands are up, and I see one blue dot and one red dot, then the guy with the red dot must raise his hand because he sees a red dot somewhere, and that can only mean that he sees it on my head, which would mean that I have a red dot on my head. But neither A nor B say anything, which means that they cannot be as sure as they would be if they saw a blue dot on my head. If they do not see a blue dot on my head, then they see a red dot. So I have a red dot on my forehead.'

7. Keep the first bulb switched on for a few minutes. The bulb should get warm. Now switch it off, switch another light on

and go upstairs. One light will be on, one bulb will be cold and one bulb will be warm.

8. First, both children go across together. One of them (let's assume it's the son) comes back alone. Then one adult (let's assume it's the mother) goes over. The daughter comes back. The son and daughter go over together. The son comes back. The dad goes over and the daughter comes back. The son and daughter go over and the son comes back. The fisherman goes over and the daughter comes back. The daughter and son go over together and give the boat back to the fisherman. The boat crosses the river 13 times in total.

9. No, the answer is not first and second. The answer is 'whole' and 'half'. This is not a list of ordinal numbers but a list of inverse fractions of natural numbers. That is, 1, 1/2, 1/3, 1/4, etc.

10. No, it's not the letter E, it is the letter F. When you place the letter F on the line, it forms the letter E.

Exercise 4: What comes next?****

1. D is the answer. Blocks 1 and 2 repeat in blocks 5 and 6.

2. C is the answer. The black square moves diagonally from the bottom right corner to the top left corner and repeats from the bottom left corner to the top right corner. The grey square moves three paces to the left in every block.

3. B is the answer. The heart and the circle move in a clockwise direction, alternating between outside and inside while the square moves one step anticlockwise and back to its original position, alternating between inside and outside.

4. D is the answer. All inside pictures move in a clockwise direction, jumping two corners. The pattern continues from Block 4 onwards but in solid shapes.

5. A is the answer. The small black dot alternates between

moving one square forward and two squares back. The small white dot alternates between one square back and two squares forward. The large black circle alternates between three squares back and two squares forward while the large white circle alternates between moving one square forward and two squares back.

6. C is the answer. The dots in each row move one step in an anticlockwise direction while the dots in each column move one step in a clockwise direction.

7. B is the answer. Sequence: mountain, valley, road through valley, valley, mountain, road through mountain.

8. D is the answer. Block 4 is the mirror image of Block 1. Block 5 is the mirror image of Block 2 and D is the mirror image of Block 3.

9. E is the answer. The solid square moves one step in a clockwise direction. The hollow circle and solid dot move anticlockwise every three squares.

10. B is the answer. If each solid circle = 1, each heart = 2 and each small square = 3, then column 1 + column 2 = column 3. The same rule applies to rows.

CHAPTER 3

Analyse This

Exercise 1: Elementary, My Dear Watson*

1. The car was a convertible. At the time of the murder, the hood of the car was down. Once the man was murdered, the murderer raised the hood, locking the man inside.

2. Turn the note upside down and you find that the numbers are actually words and sentences! They read, 'Bill is boss. He sells oil.'

3. If Thomas was attacked from behind, he could not have

noticed the attacker's V-neck sweater since the V-neck is at the front of the sweater!

4. The number on your forehead could either be a 1 (2 + 1 = 3) or a 5 (2 + 3 = 5) but if the number was one, the man with the number 3 on his forehead would immediately guess his number correctly. Since he was quiet, the answer is 5.

5. You arrest the newspaper man. You notice that only one newspaper—Monday's newspaper—was on the porch, not Tuesday's as well. The newspaperman did not bother delivering Tuesday's newspaper because he knew that the gentleman was dead.

6. The numbers 11-10-3-8-12-9 correspond to each month of the year. Therefore, the number 11 stands for the eleventh month, which is November, 10 stands for October, 3 stands for March, etc. When you take the first letter of each month, you get NOMADS. Therefore, the nomads are the murderers.

7. At the time of World War I, nobody could have known that it would be the first of the two world wars and therefore it was not named 'World War I' at that time.

8. The poison was in the ice in the fruit punch. Since the fruit punch was freshly made and the man was thirsty enough to gulp it down, the ice did not have time to melt. However, subsequently, the ice melted and the people at the party drank the fruit punch slowly, so they all got poisoned.

9. Windows can get fogged only from the inside, not outside, therefore Edith could not have wiped it off from the outside. She already knew that Margaret was dead.

10. The murderer is Ross. The victim is George. Ricky is not the murderer because he is the brother of the murderer. Sam can't be the murderer since he ran a marathon, and the murderer recently had his leg amputated, and wouldn't be able to run a marathon. Kevin is not the murderer if he just met Ricky,

since Ricky and the murderer grew up together. This leaves Ross and George. George did not grow up with Ricky since he was a farmer before moving to the big city so he cannot be the murderer. Ross is still alive (he is going to install a new computer next week) and therefore must be the murderer. It has been determined that Ricky, Sam and Ross are all alive. Kevin must also be alive since Ross plans to install Kevin's computer next week. This means that George is dead and was murdered by Ross.

Exercise 2: Shorthand**

1. 26 Letters of the Alphabet
2. 7 Wonders of the World
3. 12 Signs of the Zodiac
4. 52 Cards in a Pack (Without Jokers)
5. 1000 Years in a Millennium
6. 90° in a Right-angle Triangle
7. 3 Blind Mice (See How They Run)
8. 29 Days in February in a Leap Year
9. 13 Loaves in a Baker's Dozen
10. 9 Lives of a Cat

Exercise 3: Decoding Riddles***

a) Why can't you keep a clock in jail?
   Because time is always running out!
b) What hired killer never goes to jail?
   An exterminator!
c) Where do mummies swim?
   In the Dead Sea!
d) How long should doctors practise medicine?
   Until they get it right!

e) What is the laziest part of a car?
   The wheels! They're always tired (tyred).
f) Why did the thief steal a deck of playing cards?
   He heard there were 13 diamonds in it!
g) When is a gun unemployed?
   When it is fired!
h) What has four legs and flies?
   A picnic table!
i) Where does a calf eat?
   In a calf-eteria!
j) Where do cars swim?
   In a carpool!

Exercise 4: Einstein's Riddle****

	House 1	House 2	House 3	House 4	House 5
Colour	Yellow	Blue	Red	Green	White
Nationality	Norwegian	Dane	Brit	German	Swede
Drink	Water	Tea	Milk	Coffee	Beer
Cigarette	Dunhill	Blends	Pall Mall	Prince	Blue Master
Pet	Cats	Horses	Birds	Fish	Dogs

Answer: The German owns the fish.

CHAPTER 4

Word's Worth

Exercise 1: Word Games*

1. a) Widow
   b) Shuns
   c) Medium
   d) Civic

e) Typist
f) Literal
g) Noun
h) Reindeer
i) Notion
j) Going

2. a) sword fish/ fish finger
   b) sweetcorn/ cornflake
   c) playboy/ boyfriend
   d) honeymoon/ moonbeam
   e) somebody/ body armour
   f) catwalk/ walk out
   g) birdseed/ seedless
   h) freehand/ handcuffed
   i) sirloin/ loincloth
   j) oversleep/ sleepless

3. a) Alabama
   b) Colorado
   c) Delaware
   d) Illinois
   e) Idaho
   f) Maine
   g) Nevada
   h) Ohio
   i) Oregon
   j) Texas

4. a) JESSICA JONES
   b) SPIDERMAN
   c) WOLVERINE
   d) DEADPOOL
   e) IRONMAN
   f) AVENGERS

g)   LUKE CAGE
h)   BLACK PANTHER
i)   CAPTAIN AMERICA
j)   WASP

Exercise 2: Anagram Scramble**

1. Afghanistan
2. Seychelles
3. Bangladesh
4. Cambodia
5. Ethiopia
6. Indonesia
7. Luxembourg
8. Madagascar
9. Netherlands
10. Romania

Exercise 3: Across Words***

1. BACKSTAB
   ABDUCTED
   EDUCATES
   ESPRESSO
   SOLITUDE
   DECLINED
   EDITIONS
2. a) P
   b) Pi
   c) Pie
   d) Pine
   e) Spine
   f) Snipes
   g) Pansies

3. a)

b)

c)

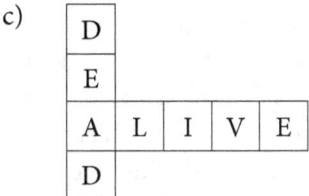

4. a) Buzzwords, buzzword, bourds, bourd, bords, bowrs, brods, brows, budos, burds, dorbs, drubs, zobus, bods, bord, bors, bowr, bows, brod, bros, brow, brus, budo, buds, orbs, robs, rubs, sorb, swob, urbs, zobu.

b) Maximised, misaimed, admixes, immixed, maidism, mismade, amides, axised, deixis, imides, maimed, medias, mesiad, sammed, admix, aides, aimed, amide, amids, amies, aside, dames, damme, deism, dimes, dime, disme, dixie, ideas, imide, imids, maids, mased, maxed, meads, media, medii, midis, mimed, mixed, aide, aids, amid, axed, daes, dais, dame, dams, desi, dies, dims, disa, dixi, idea, idem, ides, imid, made, mads, maid, meads, meds, midi, mids, sade, sadi, said, sida, side.

c) Squeezing, genies, genius, seeing, signee, eigne, genes, genie, genus, guise, negus, segni, segue, sengi, siege, singe, squeg, suing, using, zings, zing, egis, engs, euge, gees, geez, gene, gens, genu, gien, gies, gins, gnus, gues, guns, negs, sign, sing, snig, snug, sung, zigs.

5. a) Super
   b) Multi
   c) Over

Exercise 4: Word Boxes****

1. Zigzagged, zigzag, zagged, gazed, gaze, aged, gizz.

2. Subjectively, subjective, subject, leucite, levite, lucite, evict, evite, bluey, cite, bley, blue, cels, cite, cive, cubs, cub, ecus, etic, juve, luce, sley, slub, slue, tice, vice, vite, yule.

3. Absentmindedness, absentminded, mindednesses, mindedness, bemadden, beadinesses, beadiness, madness, beadmen, badness, dimnesses, dimness, madden, midden, badmen, beaded, mantids, enamine, santim, sadden, anti, mantid, bemas, denims, denim, bean, adenines, mabes, beams, beam, mint, mine, seam, mean, messan, masses, damn, amide, messes, admen, admit, dint, beads, base, time, times, edit, bams, sabe, absent, ament, sadness, sane, mane, manes, adenine, nine, bema, menad, basses, dedan, dimes, dime, dames, dame, meant, masse, minas, minae, mines, mesas, made, dines, dine, mead, mads, tided, tide, bead, semi, bads, amids, amid, bade, baded, names, name, nemas, nabes, nided, sabes, dabs, amen, anime, mids, minded, mind, sass, bam, banes, bane, bent, mesa, tines, tine, bani, mess, mass, bass, amin, dams, nabs, nebs, nabe, nema, emit, mina, smit, sabs, same, nims, means, assent, tineas, sade, adit, dint.

CHAPTER 5

Figure It Out

Exercise 1: Simple Math*

1. 60 per cent is black (9/15 x 100) and 40 per cent is yellow (6/15 x 100)
2. Square root of 3 = 1.73. Cube root of 5 = 1.70. Therefore, the cube root of 5 is the lower number.
3. 220 (A = 1) Therefore, 10+9+8+7+6+5+4+3+2+1 = 55. 55 x four suits = 220.
4. 33 (divisible by 3) and 143 (divisible by 11).
5. 11 x 12 x 13 = 1716
6.

2	4	3	1
3	1	2	4
4	3	1	2
1	2	4	3

7. 59 pairs of socks. (3 x 19 = 57 and 5 x 11 = 55)
8. Sophie works on 1 December (Tuesday), 3 December (Thursday), 5 December (Saturday), 7 December (Monday) and so on. Stephie works on 2 December (Wednesday), 5 December (Saturday) and 8 December (Tuesday). Therefore, the overlapping day is 5 December, which is a Saturday.
9. 33 is the answer. Multiply the first two digits and add the third digit.

    852 : 42 (8 x 5 + 2)

    756 : 36 (7 x 5 + 6)

    469 : 33 (4 x 6 + 9)

10. The numbers 12 and 13 need to be swapped. The top sequence goes like this: -1, -2, -1, -2, -1 and so on while the bottom sequence goes like this: -2, -1, -2, -1, -2, and so on.

Exercise 2: Deadly Sequences**

1. 7238 (it's the same number except that the numerals keep moving one place to the right.)

2. 53 (The sequence is a palindrome—the numbers read the same backwards and forwards.)

3. 0 and 50. (First digit of first number x second digit of first number = second number. First number + second number = third number and so on. Therefore, 5 X 0 = 0 and 50 + 0 = 50)

4. 22 is the answer. (First digit of number x second digit of number + third digit of number. Therefore 8 x 2 + 6 = 22)

5. 425 is the answer. (The middle number is deducted from each number. Therefore 427 – 2 = 425)

6. 214 and 107. (First number x 3 + 1 = second number, second number $\div$ 2 = third number, third number x 3 + 1 = fourth number, fourth number $\div$ 2 = fifth number etc. Therefore, 71 x 3 + 1 = 214 and 214 $\div$ 2 = 107).

7. 437 is the answer. (7 x 11 = 77, 11 x 13 = 143, 13 x 17 = 221, 17 x 19 = 323, 19 x 23 = 437)

8. 168 is the answer. Subtract 4, then multiply each number by 3 to give the next number.

9. 3413 is the answer ($1^1 = 1$, $1^1 + 2^2 = 5$, $1^1 + 2^2 + 3^3 = 32$, $1^1 + 2^2 + 3^3 + 4^4 = 288$, $1^1 + 2^2 + 3^3 + 4^4 + 5^5 = 3413$).

10. 675 is the answer (First number squared – second number = third number, third number squared – fourth number = fifth number and so on. Therefore, $27^2 – 54 = 675$).

Exercise 3: Questioning Question Marks***

1. The answer is 97. The first number on the top right corner is the sum of the first two digits of the number at the top left corner. The second number on the top right corner is the sum of second and third digits of the number on the top left corner. The same rule is applied to the bottom row.

2. The answer is 2. Logic: Bottom left square x top right square = bottom right square and top left square. Therefore, 6 x 7 = 42 (4 and 2).

3. Starting from the first column and going down and coming back up on the right column, letters advance in twos. Therefore, the missing letters are F and T.

4. The missing number is 2. Add the top rows. Add the bottom rows. Subtract the bottom row from the top row to get the number at the centre.

5. The answer is 6. In each column, the number on the top row, divided by the number on the middle row gives you the answer in the bottom row.

6. The answer is 146. In each outer square, you square all the three numbers and add them up to get the fourth number in the inner square.

7. The answer is 20. (Left square x right square) ÷ (Top square x bottom square) = 4 for all blocks.

8. The numbers on the right are 14, 25, 20, 31, 24, 17. The relationship between top and bottom rows is that you subtract the number 1 from every even number and add the number 1 to every odd number.

9. The answer is 2. The sum of each square is 33.

10. The answer is 329. Top row + middle row = bottom row.

Exercise 4: Placement Puzzles****

1. Shady Image

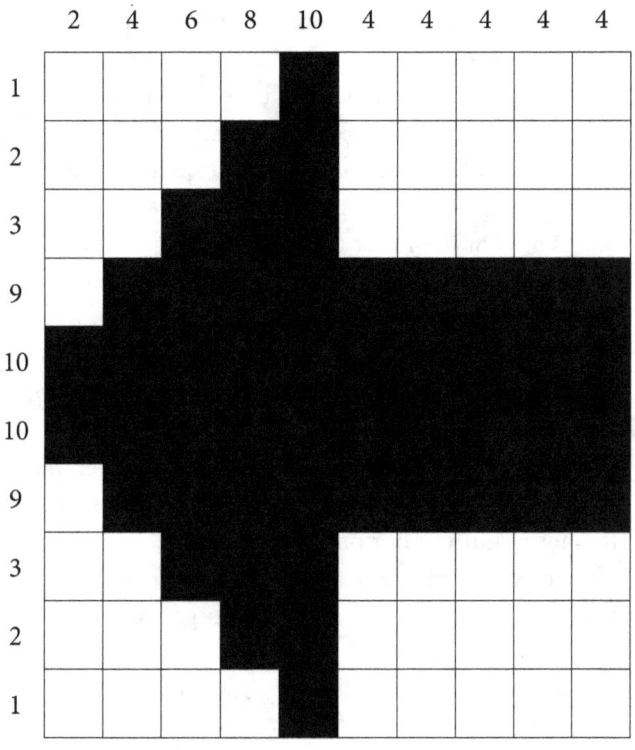

2. Pathways

61	60	2	3	4	5	9	10
64	62	59	1	6	19	8	11
35	63	58	57	20	7	18	12
36	34	56	32	22	21	17	13
38	37	33	55	31	23	16	14
39	41	42	48	54	30	24	15
40	43	47	53	49	25	29	28
44	45	46	52	51	50	26	27

3. Reverse Minesweeper

■	1		■	1			1		
2		2		2			■	2	
■	3	■	2	■	1	2	■		
	■	2		2			2		1
			1	■				■	1
					3	■		1	
		2		3	■	2			
■	4	■	■	■	2			2	
2	■	■	4	2			2	■	
		2					■	4	■

4. Infinite lines:

5. Carpeting

CHAPTER 9

Space Sense

Exercise 1: Assembling Cubes*

Unfolded cubes 4, 5, 6, 8, 10 and 12 can be folded to form cubes.

Exercise 2: Matchstick Moves**

1.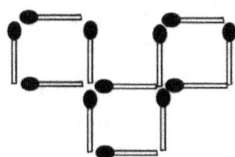

2.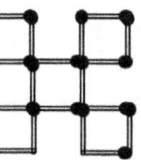

3.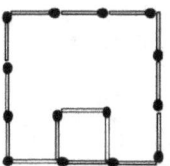

4.

5.

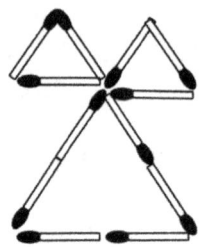

Exercise 3: Miscellaneous***

1. The bottom left cog will turn anti-clockwise while all the other cogs will turn clockwise.

2. C

3. A

4.

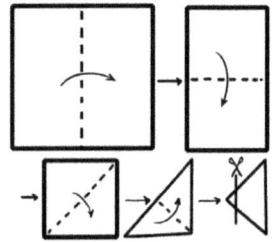

5. Let the 2-litre bottle = A, the 5-litre bottle = B and the 7-litre bottle = C.

    Step 1 – Fill up B. You will now have 0-5-2 in A, B and C respectively.

    Step 2 – Fill up A from B. You will now have 2-3-2 in A, B and C respectively.

    Step 3 – Pour A into C. You will now have 0-3-4 in A, B and C respectively.

    Step 4 – Pour B into A. You will now have 2-1-4 in A, B and C respectively.

Step 5 – Pour A into C. You will now have 0-1-6.

6. Arrange three coins touching each other at the bottom and one coin at the top like this:

7. Top view   Front view   Right view

8. B
9. A and C; B and F; D and E are identical.
10. B

Exercise 4: Mirror Images**

1.

2.

3.

4.

5.

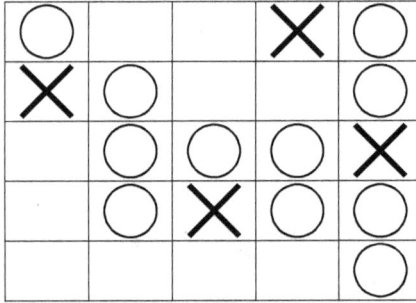